Little Owl

by Jillian Powell

Illustrated by Tomislav Zlatic

FRANKLIN WATTS

LONDON · SYDNEY

Notes on the series

TIDDLERS are structured to provide support for children who are starting to read on their own. The stories may also be used for sharing with children.

Starting to read alone can be daunting. **TIDDLERS** help by listing the words in the book for a check before reading, and by providing visual support and repeating words and phrases. These books will both develop confidence and encourage reading and rereading for pleasure.

If you are reading this book with a child, here are a few suggestions:

1. Make reading fun! Choose a time to read when you and the child are relaxed and have time to share the story.
2. Talk about the story before you start reading. Look at the cover and the blurb. What might the story be about? Why might the child like it?
3. Look also at the list of words below - can the child tackle most of the words?
4. Encourage the child to retell the story, using the jumbled picture puzzle.
5. Give praise! Remember that small mistakes need not always be corrected.

Here is a list of the words in this story.

Common words:

a	go	saw
at	it's	the
big	just	then
but	little	to
don't	look	too
down	on	up
fly	said	was

Other words:

clapped	learning	sky
flapped	looked	try
flew	owl	
high	shrew	

Little Owl was
learning to fly.

Big Owl said,
"Go on, just try!"

4

Little Owl flapped.

Big Owl clapped.

"It's just too high!"
said Little Owl.

10

"Don't look down!

Look up at the sky!"

But Little Owl
looked down.

Little Owl saw a shrew.

19

Then Little Owl flew!

Puzzle Time

a

b

Can you find these
pictures in the story?

Which pages are the pictures from?

Turn over for answers!

Answers

The pictures come
from these pages:

a. pages 16–17

b. pages 6–7

c. pages 20–21

d. pages 4–5

First published in 2014 by
Franklin Watts
338 Euston Road
London
NW1 3BH

Franklin Watts Australia
Level 17/207 Kent Street
Sydney
NSW 2000

Text © Jillian Powell 2014
Illustration © Tomislav Zlatic 2014

The rights of Jillian Powell to be
identified as the author and Tomislav Zlatic
as the illustrator of this Work have been
asserted in accordance with the Copyright,
Designs and Patents Act, 1988.

A CIP catalogue record for this book is
available from the British Library.

ISBN 978 1 4451 3266 2 (hbk)
ISBN 978 1 4451 3268 6 (pbk)
ISBN 978 1 4451 3265 5 (ebook)
ISBN 978 1 4451 3267 9 (library ebook)

Series Editor: Jackie Hamley
Editor: Melanie Palmer
Series Advisor: Catherine Glavina
Series Designer: Peter Scoulding

Printed in China

Franklin Watts is a division of Hachette Children's Books,
an Hachette UK company. www.hachette.co.uk